Deadly Sins: Greed

Chapter One

Older Women Make Beautiful Lovers

It's not that he was greedy, but in his family, there was a certain expectation. One he would soon realize older women could help him attain.

"Hey, what're you doing?" Chad asked, leaning against a light pole. "You're drunk."

"No, you're drunk!" His friend Jax replied.

"Oh, I know I'm drunk," Chad said. "Here." He stumbled off the curb into the edge of the road, jumping like a madman. Jax looked around to see if anyone else was watching the show and was just about to pull his friend back on the sidewalk when the taxi pulled over.

"You really want to take a taxi home?" Jax asked. "It's an hour drive. Without traffic."

"Nah," Chad said, opening the door and getting in when his friend wouldn't. "We can crash at my mom's." He gave the driver the address to his mom's condo and waited while his friend fell into the car.

Jax would've stayed half laid out on the seat and the floor board for the whole trip, but the driver angrily scowled at them through the rearview mirror until he was upright and buckled. "Won't your mom be upset?" Jax was winded from the effort sitting upright in a car correctly took out of him. "I mean she won't be too happy when we show up in this condition."

"Don't worry about it. She's in Spain."

"Spain!" Jax stared straight ahead wide eyed. "Must be nice. Wait. I thought she didn't get as much in that settlement as she expected."

"She didn't," Chad told him. "She's on her honeymoon." He was snickering before the word was out of his mouth, making it hard to say it.

"Honeymoon? Are you kidding me? What is this now? Like five or six?"

Chad had a hard time answering. Every time he opened his mouth, he couldn't stop laughing. "Eight," he finally answered.

"God damn!" Jax shouted. "Sorry, bro, but your mom gets more ass than the two of us put together."

The taxi pulled up to the building, and Chad paid him, giving him a tip which was probably larger than he intended. Counting was proving difficult. They fell out of the car with little help from the doorman.

"Good to see you again, sir," the doorman told Chad. "Looks like it's been a good night."

He quite often crashed at his mom's when he was in the city, and she was out of town. Having her gone made the visits tolerable. "My buddy's getting married in two weeks!" Chad grabbed his friend's shoulders and shook him gently. "No more bachelor life for him."

They went up to his mom's unit. There were only two bedrooms. Chad led his friend to the spare room, instructing him, "Whatever you do, don't get sick in here."

"I'll clean it up," Jax mumbled. He was already on the verge of passing out.

"Professionally," Chad said. "Even then, my mom will

complain about the smell for a year."

Chad made his way back down to his mother's room after stopping in the bathroom to gulp down several glasses of water and hit the head. He went in her room too drunk to worry about how many men had shared the bed with her. He stripped off all his clothes because it was so hot in her condo. The woman always kept the thermostat set at the temperature of the second circle of hell. Once he laid down and closed his eyes, he'd have been out in seconds, but he was scared sober by a woman's scream.

"Who are you?" she yelled, clutching the blanket to her neck.

"Who the hell are you?" he asked, jumping up from the bed in all his glory.

"I asked you first," she demanded.

"This is my mom's place," he said, wondering where the hell his cell phone was to call security.

"Oh," the woman relaxed. "You're Chad. I'm Dee. I'm Donald's sister."

The names meant nothing to him. "Who the hell are you?" he asked again.

"My brother is in Spain with your mom." She spoke slowly, spelling it out for him.

It took a minute for Chad to realize she was talking about his mom's new husband. He stopped remembering their names after the third one. "So why are you here?" He had calmed down, but it was becoming difficult to stay on his feet.

"I'm house sitting while they're gone."

"You know that means you come and go, right?" He really didn't have a problem with her being here, but he wasn't about to sleep on the couch. This was his mom. He got dibs on the bed.

The woman sighed and dropped the blanket, relaxing now she realized the man hadn't broke in to attack her. "She knows I'm staying here and vacationing in the city while they're gone. It's fine."

He needed to get off his feet, so he laid back down in the bed, rolling away from her.

"What are you doing?" She shook him like she thought he was already asleep.

He rolled back over. "I'm going to sleep."

"Not here, you aren't!"

"Listen. This is my mom's bed. I'm sleeping in it. You can stay or go to the couch. I don't care."

"Just go to the spare room," she said.

"Can't. My buddy's probably already covered it in puke."

"I'm not sleeping on the couch!" The woman had become irate.

"Then stay," he said, closing his eyes.

She shook him again to wake him. When his eyes opened, the city lights peeking through the blinds of the window landed on her face, softening it, and on her exposed cleavage. It was the first time he caught a glimpse of the nightie she was wearing.

"Damn, baby," he crooned. "You're looking fine as hell," he said, reaching to caress the side of her face with his fingers.

Dee slapped his hand away. "I'm old enough to be your mother. And you're drunk," she spat.

"Drunk still needs to fuck, and age still gets laid, right? Maybe we can help each other out."

She tried everything to discourage him, but he kept making passes. She'd have gone to the couch, but her back would kill her tomorrow if she did. Worst of all, her nether regions were enjoying his flirtatious comments. It'd been years since she'd been this close to a man. It didn't take her long to get over the moral right or wrong dilemma. This guy's mom was after her brother to take him for every dime he had, but Donald was too blind to see it. Fair is fair.

"Alright," she said, surprising him. "But I warn you. You'll never want one of those young girls you're used to messing around with again." She leaned over and gave him a feather light peck on the lips.

"Are you sure you won't have regrets in the morning?" He didn't really care, but today's age demanded giving a woman a second chance to change her mind.

"How old are you?" she asked.

"Twenty-four."

"No regrets then. But, you're the one who's gonna face a day where you'll think none of this would've happened if I'd never slept with Dee."

"Whatever," he said, propping up on one elbow to pull her down to him.

They kissed long and passionately. He pulled her nightie over her head, with help. His hands fumbled not doing what he wanted. She held her arms out to him, and he scrambled into her embrace. They kissed again, and he nuzzled her neck.

His hands traced down her chest and found her elegant, but small breasts. Each with a large rock hard nipple protruding from it. He tongued them individually, given them equal concentration.

He continued his attention downward, nibbling and licking her entire abdomen, kissing his way down to her small triangle of hair. He moved into position between her legs, swaying back and forth with the room which always wanted to be slightly off tilt. He kissed the inside of her thighs, slowly making his way to the folds of her womanhood.

Dee was moaning her approval, encouraging him.

As he drew near her center, he kissed her outer lips, sucking one then the other. "Mmm," she moaned. He believed she was enjoying his show.

His mouth found her clit, and he flicked the tip of it with his tongue. He circled it round and round until the sounds he heard from her were a series of grunts. Her body shuddered, and her legs began to shake.

"Like that, huh?" he asked.

"I know how to work my body," she said.

The comment confused him at the time and was quickly forgotten. It wouldn't be long until another woman taught him exactly what that meant.

He pulled himself forward to position his hard cock, but she stopped him.

"Allow me," she said, gently pushing his shoulders and guiding him to his back next to her. "I don't think you have it in you."

Chad wanted to object, but he had to stop the room from spinning first.

She straddled him and reached for his cock with one hand while bracing her other hand against his shoulder for support. She guided it to her entrance and held it while she slid down.

"Oh, fuck, yeah," Chad grunted. He lifted up and brought his mouth back to her breast. There was a sudden intake of air when she took his full length and grinded hard into the base of his shaft.

Dee's tunnel closed around him, gripping him like magical fingers inside her labyrinth. It felt like a massage with every stroke.

It was the best pussy he'd ever had. He couldn't focus on her breasts, so he laid back, letting her fuck the hell out of him. The only thing on his mind was not wanting to cum too fast when he could normally last a couple hours at least.

She fucked him fierce. Sometimes coming down hard like she wanted more. Others times grinding into his base, back and forth, side to side, in circles. She did everything. But his favorite was when she took him deep, arching her back, then rocked back and forth in slow movements as her pussy clutched his cock tightly.

"I'm almost there," she whispered.

Chad gripped her hips, not realizing he'd been dead, drunk weight for most of it until her voice made him pay attention. He opened her eyes and saw her. Her head was tilted back, and she was rolling her nipples between her finger tips. Her orgasm was electrifying his cock with wave after wave of pleasure. When she licked her lips, he lost it.

His cock began to twitch out of his control, pulling his load from his balls to shoot deep in her box. "Damn!" he practically shouted. He couldn't remember the last time he came that fast.

Dee smiled sweetly at him and rocked his cock slowly until he was spent. She lifted herself off him and stood up, pulling her nightie over her head again. "I'm going to clean up," she said. "Want a glass of water?"

"Yeah," he said. He was out by the time she returned.

The next morning he woke up alone in the bed. His memories were fuzzy, but he remembered the woman he had slept with last night.

He stumbled out into the kitchen after checking on Jax who was snoring like a lumberjack and using the bathroom. There she was, standing in the kitchen, pouring coffee in a travel mug. She wasn't a dream after all.

It was the first really good look he had of her. There was a little pudge in the middle which he didn't mind at all. Her ass was round for an older woman. Usually sometime between children heading off to college and their fiftieth birthday, a woman's ass runs away. No one really understands where it goes. He was trying to sneak up behind her, to grab her around the waist, and have some breakfast. The one thing he remembered clearly was the sex had been awesome.

His foot hit the leg of the stool by the kitchen island and gave him away. Dee turned around, and he almost screamed. Even with the layers of makeup caked on her face, he could see the wrinkles and skin sag she was trying to hide. The sight went straight to his head, making his hangover pound out all the reasons why every time he drinks, he swears he'll never drink that much again only to do it the next time.

'This can't be the same woman. Dee was a goddess. Barely my mother's age. This woman could be my grandmother!'

"Good morning." She smiled at him like the thought of having breakfast together had crossed her mind too.

He swallowed hard, feeling last night's drinks trying to come up. If she made a move to touch him, he worried it might win the fight, and he'd get sick all over her.

"I was going to fix you guys some breakfast, but I didn't know when you'd be up. Plus, I'm sure you're feeling it today."

All Chad could do was nod. If he tried to speak, the flood

gates would open, and the kitchen would be covered in vomit.

"Well, I'm off," she said, picking up her purse. "Maybe I'll see you again before your mother gets back. We can go to Charley's. My treat. You know where to find me." She winked at him and blew him a kiss before walking out the door.

After she left, he scrubbed himself in the shower. He was thankful Jax was still passed out. No one could ever find out about this drunken one night stand. The teasing would follow him as long as he lived. Still, he had to admit the sex was amazing. It could just never be repeated now that he'd seen her in the daylight.

'You were drunk,' he told himself. He tilted his head back to rinse his hair, closing his eyes. He saw her above him. Her body softly lit from the lights of the city. He could feel the way her body rocked against his, and the memory made his cock jump in excitement.

His eyes snapped open, and he shut off the water. *'What are you doing?'* This was one woman he never imagined he'd be fantasizing about.

He dried off and put his clothes back on, wishing he had something clean with him. He smelled like alcohol and sex.

There was a loud moan from the hall. Jax was awake. He opened the door and rushed out, letting his friend get to the toilet quickly.

Back in the kitchen, he helped himself to the coffee Dee made. *'Well, they do say older women make beautiful lovers.'* Like it or not, Dee had proved that last night. *'Maybe it was just her,'* he thought. *'It doesn't mean they all know what they're doing like she did.'*

He thought about some of the older women he knew from

work or his friend's parents. Some of them had really taken care of themselves and still looked hot. Charley's was the most expensive restaurant in the city. Even his own parents didn't go there, and they had money to blow. If Dee was willing to lay down that kind of cash for another helping of a younger man, he wondered what other older women might offer.

Chapter Two

Firecracker at Fifty

Chad wouldn't say he was taking advantage of these women because if anything, they're taking advantage of the opportunity to have someone half their age in bed. Through Maggie, he learned two things. Older women are amazing in the sack. It wasn't a one-time fluke with Dee. They were also very giving in other ways.

He'd been thinking about Dee from the bachelor party to the wedding. Not so much the woman herself, but the sex. He wanted to test out his theory. He wanted to see if all older women were great in bed, and if they would all treat him to some other perks as well.

During the reception, he noticed a woman who came alone. She was always with a group of friends, and there wasn't a man in sight. He guessed her to be in her late thirties, and she was damn good looking with legs for days. All he could think about was getting them wrapped around him.

The problem was getting her alone. These friends of hers were practically joined to her waist. It was pissing him off. He'd been so busy helping his buddy out, fulfilling his duties as best man, even stepping up and helping his friend's fiancé by picking up her family from the airport. He hadn't had a minute to himself to prowl. Now this hot woman was dancing twenty feet away, and her friends were cock blocking him. He wanted to approach her alone because he had learned enough in life to know not everyone was tolerant of age differences.

When he saw her slip away, the night was far from over. Surprisingly, her friends stuck around at the reception instead of leaving with her. He followed her outside where she gave her ticket to the valet. As soon as he walked her way, she fumbled with something in her purse and dropped it. Chad rushed in to help.

"Thank you so much," she said sweetly.

"Always willing to help a beautiful lady," he said.

She gave him the eye and giggled. "Oh, stop."

He handed her the card which had fallen out. It was a fiftieth birthday card. "Here. Someone you know turning the big five-oh soon?" he asked.

"Me," she said.

"Not a chance." This woman couldn't be a day older than forty. *'Note to self: Don't stick around till morning when she's not wearing make-up.'*

She nodded. "It's my birthday today."

"The night's still young. Why leave so soon?"

"At my age, the nights keep getting shorter."

He flashed her his best come hither smile.

"You're sweet," she said, "but a handsome man like you could have any woman in there. Why bother with an old lady like me?"

Chad had learned there were three types of responses from women. Some women shoot you down straight away. Some enjoy the attention. It's the ones who flirt back who are interested even if they're not completely sure how far they're willing to go. All he had to do now was find out if she'd carry it through.

"I don't see an old lady when I look at you. I see a beautiful vision who must be lying about her age."

Her cheeks flushed dark red. "I'd sleep with you," she said. Her eyes seductively stared into his soul. "But you'd fall in love."

The car pulled up, and the driver opened the door for her. "Well enjoy the rest of the party," she said with a wave.

"Oh, I'm done too. Just got to call for my ride," he said. Then he added, "Unless…" letting the word draw out of his mouth.

She looked at him, really studied him, and then finally said, "Alright. I'll drive you home."

It wasn't quite the answer he was hoping for, but it gave him more time to work his magic.

They made their introductions as they drove off. Her name was Maggie. She was a receptionist at a daycare who could never have children herself. He told her he worked for State Mutual Insurance which was true, but he left out the part about his grandfather being the one who built the company from the ground up.

Two blocks away, she started saying, "I can't believe I'm doing this," and shaking her head. "I'm too old for this."

That's when Chad knew she wasn't driving him back to his apartment. They were going to her place.

She pulled into a circle drive in front of a gorgeous two story home. There was a high price tag attached to this neighborhood. *'Must be divorce earned,'* he joked to himself. Women tended to come out high on the hog in divorce settlements. He should know. His mother traded up all the time.

He followed her into the house and let her pour him a drink. When she brought it to him, he wrapped his arm around her waist, pulling her tightly to him.

Maggie's eyes closed, and she inhaled deeply. "What am I doing?" she asked quietly. Then she opened her eyes and brought her lips to his.

Once in the bedroom, she was even more of a firecracker than Dee had been. Either Maggie was more experienced, or he was paying attention better because he hadn't drank as much tonight.

She took complete control, stripping him naked and stroking his cock before even unzipping her dress. When he tried to help, she pushed him back on the bed.

Chad watched while she slowly undressed. Her body looked more weathered than her face, not having cosmetics to cover the flaws. It didn't make her less beautiful. In fact, he found it even more attractive which surprised him. It was like a map of the life she had lived, telling her story on her body. He wanted to kiss and lick every mar on her skin.

"I'm not much into foreplay," she told him, standing nude next to the bed. "I know what I like, but if you want it..."

He smiled and shook his head. "You know how to work your body, huh?" he smiled, repeating what Dee had said.

Maggie's head went back in surprise. "Yeah, that's right. Ready?"

"Yes, please."

She straddled him. He wondered if it was a coincidence, or if there was something about older women wanting to take control. It didn't make a difference to him. He was getting laid either way.

Chad sat on the edge of the bed with Maggie on his lap. He gripped her ass to support her, and she whispered in his ear to give it a smack. "Not too hard," she instructed.

He brought his hand down across one cheek, and she moaned. "Just like that."

She lifted up and caught the tip of his cock with the entrance to his tunnel, and slowly slid him inside her.

'Damn,' he thought. *'She's fucking tight.'* Divorced. Fifty. He imagined she hadn't been fucked for a while, maybe even years.

It was like being with Dee all over again. Maggie's pussy gripped his cock. It tightened and relaxed, massaging his stiff member. It was almost like a hand job and a fuck rolled into one, and it drove him crazy.

She'd fuck him for several strokes then come down hard, grinding against him while leaning back as far as her arms would stretch. Her hands rested on his shoulders, keeping her from falling. Every minute or two, he'd smack her ass, and she'd cry out softly.

Her first orgasm almost caused him to buckle. It felt like fireworks exploding around his cock. *'How do older women do it? I can definitely tell she's not faking it.'* The thought began a nightmare playing in his head of wondering if he'd ever made a woman truly cum before Dee. He pushed it out of his head for now, but it'd play on repeat at the worst times for months.

"I want you to come," she whispered in his ear.

His cock jerked at the words.

"Is it that easy? Just say it, and you obey?"

He grabbed her and bucked into her from underneath. In seconds, he was cumming into her while her tunnel convulsed around his cock. Her moans described her second climax.

She climbed off him and laid down with her eyes shut. Her breathing was deep, and the smile on her face wasn't leaving any time soon.

Chad wasn't sure what move to make next. He reached for his clothes then stopped. "What do you want? Should I go?"

"You don't have to run out so quickly," she said. "Take your time."

He laid down next to her and draped an arm over her waist. She opened her eyes and looked at him. "Hi," he said.

Maggie giggled, and it made him smile. "Oh, the things you never thought you'd do," she said.

After a little while, he got up and dressed. If he stayed there any longer, he'd have fallen asleep. "Can I see you again?" he asked.

"Didn't I say you'd fall in love?" she laughed, climbing out of bed.

"Not in love," he said. "But I would like to see you again."

It looked like she wasn't going to answer. She was taking so long that if she did say anything, he believed it would be simply to shoot him down.

"Let me get you an Uber," she said, picking up her phone. "Address?"

He gave it to her, and a minute later she said, "There. And it's paid."

They walked downstairs to wait for the car. "You never answered me," he told her.

The look on her face said rejection was coming, but then it changed. "Fine. She left the room and returned with a slip of paper. "This is my work number. You can call me there, but don't abuse it. That's my job on the line."

"Why not just give me your cell number?"

Maggie laughed at him like it was an absurd idea. "Because my husband might get suspicious of the strange calls listed on the bill."

Internally, Chad felt like he stumbled backward with his mouth on the floor. He managed to keep it together in front of her although he wasn't sure how he accomplished that feat. *'She's married! Fuck!'*

"Where is he now?" It never crossed his mind a jealous husband might have barged in on them while they had sex.

"Oh, he's at a golf tournament out of state," she shrugged. "Him and his golf," she said, rolling her eyes.

He went home thinking he'd never see her again, never call. There were many things about him that people would look down on, but married women were off the table. He saw the affairs too many times with his parents' marriages, all of their combined marriages, to do something like that himself. At least he wouldn't do it intentionally. From now on, he'd make sure to ask if they were single first instead of assuming they wouldn't be taking him home if they weren't.

During the ride home, he became even angrier. The last thing he needed was a scandal before he could collect his money. He didn't want to do anything to step on his dad's or granddad's toes before the funds were in his account. It'd be several years before he had it all. Trust funds. His granddad's will. The promotion at work he had to prove himself to get. It was his granddad who insisted children work for it instead of being spoiled. That's why he lived in a bare apartment and worked a menial desk job at the insurance company. It was all to prove he could make it without the family money before they let him have the family money.

It wasn't enough to make him give up on older woman just yet. He was going to find a sugar momma one way or the other. There was a certain lifestyle he was accustomed too with his upbringing, and he didn't make near enough yet to afford it on his own. Next time, he'd ask if they were married. Obviously noticing the lack of a wedding band wasn't enough. He also considered giving a fake name just in case she lied, and her husband came looking for the guy having an affair with his wife.

He was still a little buzzed and getting very tired. It was late, and the only thing he wanted to do the rest of the night was sleep. He'd worry about getting a ride to the country club where his car was parked in the morning.

Chapter Three

He Deserves It

Chad had never thought of himself as arrogant before, but it was harder than he ever expected to find another older woman. It took three whole days. Most of the ones he flirted with looked at him like he was an extra kind of special. Some took the flattery well, but finding one who said yes? It was a blow to his ego. Ladies his age threw themselves at him.

He had a date set up for the weekend with Mel. She was divorced, and he did as much as he could to be sure of it. They were going to the city to a fancy restaurant and a traveling production of "Wicked."

Everything was moving in the right direction until he swung by the coffee shop on his way to work Wednesday morning. Hump day. It wasn't lost on him.

He opened the door and held it for an older couple headed toward it. When he looked up, he was rather surprised to make eye contact with Maggie. She was with her husband, walking arm in arm. The fact they recognized each other was obvious.

"You know this guy?" her husband asked.

"Yes," she said, patting his arm. "This is Chad. He works for our agent at State Mutual Insurance."

Chad had to bite his lip to keep from reacting. This was his granddad's insurance company. He wasn't just some flunky in an agent's office. He'd one day have a seat on the board. Of course,

Maggie didn't know that, couldn't find out that either. All he told her was the name of the company he worked for, not what he did there. He was used to people sniffing around him hoping he'd drop some of the family money, not realizing he didn't have it yet.

"Hmph," he said, tugging on his wife's arm to go inside.

He stood behind them in line, wondering how nervous Maggie must be feeling. It never occurred to him to step to the side to wait a minute and help her out. It was a good thing he didn't. If he had moved away, he'd never have witnessed what a dick her husband was. It had to be hard to greet the world with a smile considering what she dealt with from him. At least, Chad assumed his behavior at the coffee shop was typical of what her husband was like.

This man was downright rude to the employees. He called all of the baristas "honey" in that condescending, sexually objectifying way. All of them except for the one man working behind the counter. That one he grunted at and asked why he was doing a woman's job. "Can't you find manly work?"

Meanwhile, he was just as rude to his wife. He cut her off every time she tried to make conversation. And when she ordered! She got the medium sized drink, regardless of the fancy name they called it. "Are you sure?" he asked, leaning back to look at her ass. "Think there's room in those pants for it?"

It infuriated Chad when she quietly changed her order to a small with the sugar alternative. *That's it,'* he thought, making up his mind to call her that day. *'If anyone deserves to be cheated on, it's him.'*

When he told her who he was on the phone, she laughed. "Funny," she said. "I was beginning to think I'd never hear from you, but after running into you this morning, I knew you'd be calling."

"Why's that?" he asked.

"I figured either you'd be reminded of how much you enjoyed fucking me last weekend, or your guilt from ghosting me would cause you to make the call."

"I didn't ghost you," he said, knowing that's exactly what he intended on doing. "It's just I've busy catching up with everything after the wedding."

"That's right," she said. "I forgot you were the best man."

"Really?" he teased. "So you're saying I'm the best?"

It was impossible not to smile when Maggie laughed like she did after hearing that. "No," she said honestly, "but you've got potential."

Chad knew he was out of his league, sexually speaking, with her. He took it as a major compliment.

It was the beginning of a three month affair which started that night. Of course, he didn't toss away Mel either. There was enough of him to go around. He learned from them that older women were worth more than their skill in bed. They were very generous outside the bedroom too. They were more established in life. Their kids were grown if they had any. They had more money, and they loved to shower people with gifts.

He met her at a restaurant where she told her friends she had called for a car. Her husband had a weekly poker night, so they had a few hours before she would have to be home. Neither of them knew where they wanted to go. Her house was out just to be on the safe side in case he did come home early. He never did, but you know, Murphy's Law and all. His apartment was out due to sheer embarrassment. His bed consisted of a set of queen mattresses laying on the floor.

They drove down to the local park and cruised around the lake looking for the right spot. Others in the community used this place as a hook up hang out, so why not them? If Maggie had any objections to it, she kept them to herself. There was the risk of a cop coming by on patrol, but they'd just have to keep an eye out for headlights.

Maggie giggled when he chose an empty four car parking area with a burnt out street light near it. He was surprised there wasn't already a car rocking in it, but the weather was perfect. They were probably around, just outside in the trees. "Oh, I feel like a teenager again."

He leaned across the seat and kissed her passionately. This woman was amazing. She was beautiful and kept her kindness after years of being married to a jackass.

He moved from her mouth, kissing her with purpose. His lips and tongue teasing and leading to her breasts, sending tingles between her thighs. He moved his mouth to her neck, kissing her gently then her ear.

Chad whispered, "You smell so good, and you look amazing in that dress." His hand found her breasts as he spoke. With each move, he applied a little more pressure than his fingers slipped into the neckline, carefully pulling it down to reveal her lacy bra. "Your breasts are delicious," he moaned.

He lowered one cup, and said, "You have gorgeous nipples."

"Are you going to compliment every part of my body," Maggie asked.

"I might," he smiled. Before she could remind him of her no foreplay preference, he brought his mouth to her breast, teasing her nipple with his teeth.

She gently pushed him away after a moment which he expected. She reached for the waistband of his jeans and unfastened them. "Slide them down," she said, already moving to climb over.

"Here? Like this?" he asked, glancing in the backseat. The backseat he cleared out before picking her up just for this very reason.

"I like to be in the driver's seat," she said.

He slid his pants down, knowing she was being completely honest, and he didn't mind not having all the pressure on him one bit.

Maggie swung her leg over him, and they shimmied around until they were both comfortable. Chad had to extend the seat back as far as it would go. She hiked her dress up to her waist, exposing the garter belt holding up her hose, but she wore nothing else underneath.

"I like your style," he said.

Her eyes sparkled, and she took his shaft in her hand, stroking it before leading his cock to her tunnel. The second his member made contact with her moist entrance, they both moaned.

Maggie slid down his full length slowly, savoring every inch of him. It drove him mad. His cock throbbed hard, begging to be buried inside her. Once he was all the way in, he smacked her ass like she taught him. "Good boy," she whispered in his ear, increasing her rhythm to a steady tempo.

He lowered one hand from her hips and found her clit, rubbing it gently.

"That's it," she encouraged him.

Chad continued to tease her clit. In minutes, Maggie tilted

her head back. She didn't moan and scream, make a fuss like his other girlfriends had. She didn't need to. When she came, his cock was caught in the cross-fire of her pulsating labyrinth. He lifted his hips, thrusting into her the best he could in the confined space, trying to take her higher.

Once her orgasm passed, she leaned back on the steering wheel and angled herself. "There!" she practically yelled.

He drove his cock into her as hard as he could. She convulsed and shook. Her juices ran down his cock, between his legs, and dampened his seat. It went on for minutes. It was like a never ending orgasm.

Maggie threw herself forward, closer to him, growling. The fire in her eyes made her seem like a raging tiger on the hunt. She grabbed a handful of his hair and yanked his head hard to the side. "You're going to come for me," she ordered.

Chad nodded and quickened his pace. He gripped her hips and pulled her toward him as he pummeled into her. Seconds later, his body jerked with each shot of cum jutting from his cock.

She moaned and rolled over to the passenger seat. From her purse, she grabbed a small package of tissue, offering him a couple before taking more to clean herself.

"That was fun," she said, "but not something I can do every time. I prefer a bed. I've lived long enough to earn it," she laughed. "Next time, your apartment, and I'll cook."

"There's not much at my place," he admitted.

"Got a bed?"

"I have mattresses," he said.

"That's enough."

"Okay," he agreed. "What do you want to make? I'll have to

go to the store."

Maggie laughed so hard she almost cried. "I forgot how bachelors live. I bet there's nothing in the fridge except beer."

"Something like that."

"It's fine. I'll schedule a grocery delivery for whatever day we do this."

Chad drove her home and wanted so badly to follow her inside after their long kiss goodnight, but knew it was a bad idea. When he drove away, he thought for sure the driver of the car who turned onto the street looked like Maggie's husband, and he was right. It was the first of many times when they were almost caught.

When the day came, more than just the groceries for the meal arrived. Bag after bag was left at his door. There was cereal and milk, staples like soup and frozen meals. Maggie even ordered candles and toilet paper. She had thought about almost everything a bachelor pad might be lacking.

Maggie had been boasting about her culinary skills ever since the night in the park, but Chad would have to wait to find out she was telling the truth. The lasagna never did get made. Her secret family recipe for marinara sauce burnt in the pan while he fucked her against the kitchen counter. It was the best meal any woman ever cooked for him, before or since.

She ended it after one too many close calls worried about her husband finding out. Served him right anyway. He wasn't exactly where he said he was going to be when she ran into him on the pier. Both of them claimed to be out for some fresh air, but Chad saw the woman who had darted into one of the shops. Having lost his date for the night, he swooped in to take another one of the douche bag's women.

Out with the old, and in with the new. That's how he met Judy, the woman who would one day ruin his life. He was already juggling Lydia, who he was about to meet, and Mel even with Maggie's graceful exit, but he had to be greedy, had to believe he could continue to handle three affairs at once. Then he went on to double it.

Chapter Four

Being Neighborly

Lydia was just as impressive as the other older women who had entertained him. Some days he liked to think he was the one who had brought the extra spark to the affairs, but deep down he knew it wasn't true. These women had voracious appetites and a patience for teaching.

When he came home from work that unassuming Wednesday, he saw the notices plastered all over the complex. One of the massive water heaters for the building had busted. Some apartments would be without water until then, but it didn't list which ones. Due to the late hour and staff shortages, it wouldn't be fixed until the next day at the earliest. "Please be kind to your neighbors," the notes read at the bottom.

The first thing he did when he walked in the door was test the water in his kitchen. It was still hot. He exhaled a sigh of relief. He had a late date with Maggie that night while her husband played poker, so he needed to be able to wash the stench of sex off him before bed.

About an hour later, there was a knock on the door. It was Mrs. Grisham from apartment 4B at the end of the hall near the other elevator. She was a kind elderly woman who very much was the adopted grandmother of the building.

"Oh, Chad, I'm glad you're home," she said.

"How are you this evening, Mrs. Grisham? You're looking as

lovely as ever," he told her.

"Oh, you!" she cried.

He loved seeing the way her eyes lit up whenever he complimented her. She liked to play coy, but he knew she was a looker in her day.

"I need a favor," she told him. "I was hoping you could help."

"Anything," he said. Then he remembered the notices about the water heater. This must be what the note meant about being kind to neighbors. Water and gas were included in the rent which meant hot water was essentially free. "Did you want to use my shower?" he asked uncertain. It was a shot in the dark.

"Not me," she said. "My daughter is visiting and spent the day playing volleyball at the rec center." Mrs. Grisham raised her hand to her mouth like she was spilling a secret and was afraid someone would overhear. "She doesn't like to shower there."

"I can't say I blame her," Chad said.

"But then she came home, and..." Mrs. Grisham shrugged.

"It's no problem. Anything for you, my beautiful neighbor," Chad said with a gracious bow.

Mrs. Grisham's face flushed, and she waved at Chad like she was irritated by his nonsense. The beaming grin on her face said something else entirely. "I'll send her down," she said, walking away. "Thank you!"

A few minutes later, there was a second knock on the door. Chad was blown away when he answered it. The woman standing in front of him couldn't be Mrs. Grisham's daughter.

"Hi, I'm Lydia," she said smiling. When Chad didn't say anything, she added, "Mom... Mrs. Grisham... said you were okay with me showering here?"

He still couldn't speak, but he stepped aside to let her in the door. This woman had beautiful blonde hair which hung past her shoulders in bouncing waves. Her bright blue eyes sparkled, and her natural face gave away the hint of a few wrinkles, but she couldn't have been more than a decade older than him. There was no way Lydia had even reached forty yet much less the age he guessed her to be based on how old Mrs. Grisham looked.

Chad finally found his voice. "I thought Mrs. Grisham said her daughter would be by, but you must be her grand-daughter," he said.

"Mom said you were a flirt," she laughed.

The two of them chatted for several minutes before he showed her to the bathroom. He dished it out, and she served it right back. He had never been more certain a woman was into him and hot for his cock. If he had misjudged the situation, it could've led to a number of complications for him, but he didn't once stop to think about if he was wrong because he was convinced Lydia wanted to fuck him. She was just too shy? Maybe. Insecure? Doubtful. He wasn't sure, but something held her back from being forward.

He waited for a few minutes after hearing the shower curtain pull closed before opening the bathroom door. There was no key for the door, but a paperclip unlocked it easily. The click the latch made when the door shut was louder than he expected which meant his effort to be as quiet as possible was done in vain. Most of his clothes were in the hallway. All that was left to remove were his shorts and boxer briefs.

"Hello?" her voice rang out over the sound of flowing water. "Is that you Chad?"

'Shit!' He had hoped to listen to her for a while, building his courage to act. "Yes," he finally said.

"Do you need something?"

Her voice didn't sound alarmed. Taking a shower at a stranger's house had to be a little intimidating especially for a woman going into a man's bathroom she had just met. Yet, she didn't seemed bothered by his presence at all. He stripped off the rest of his clothing. He was joining her. "No, actually, I thought you might," he said.

He pulled the curtain open just enough to see she was facing away from him. She looked around at the bottles she had brought with her, making sure she had all the soaps and shampoos she needed. Meanwhile, he grabbed her body wash, squirting some from the pump into his hands and lathered them with the spray of the water.

"No, I have everything," she said loudly, thinking he was still on the other side of the curtain.

"Are you sure?" he asked.

The sound of his voice so near made her jump. She turned around and saw him leaning in the open curtain, fully nude with his hands ready to help.

"I guess not," she giggled.

Chad took that as his invitation and stepped into the tub. She pulled the curtain closed after him, coming close enough to brush her supple breasts across his chest and arm.

"Are you sure?" she asked him.

"I was about to ask you the same question."

Lydia faced away from him and lifted her hair over one shoulder, so it lay down her chest. "My back is always the hardest place to reach."

He lathered her back, massaging her as he worked. She had a picture perfect hourglass figure with a few extra pounds around the middle. Proof of the years she lived happily, taking what she wanted, and not being afraid to indulge. He loved a woman who would eat a cupcake instead of worrying about the scale.

Chad let his hands roam south to the small of her back and stepped closer. He kissed her neck soft and gently. He spread her legs open with his feet, and she moaned softly. Then he ran his hands up and down her inner thighs, ending with running them up the crack of her ass.

He turned her around and kissed her lips, silencing her moans. Her hands explored his muscular chest and abs, but when they ventured further, he stopped her. If Lydia was like the other older women he'd been with, her skill would reduce his stamina. Too much foreplay could make for a very embarrassing shower.

"I love your ass and breasts," he whispered, breaking the kiss. "Let me look at the rest of you."

Sinking to his knees, he spread her outer lips open. His tongue traveled up her folds to her clit then repeated the path several times. His lips grabbed her clit, rubbing it between them for a moment before his tongue broke free, teasing it.

He continued to rub and lick her with the water pouring over his face until it stopped. Lydia had angled the shower head to help him out. It was now cascading over his back. He inserted one finger than two, fucking her with his hand.

"I'm so wet," Lydia giggled. "Even without the shower."

Chad pulled his face back from her pussy just long enough to say. "Good. I want you to cum hard for me."

He licked her more feverishly after that. His tongue would occasionally dart down to her folds, replacing the fingers in her tunnel for a minute before moving back to her clit. He licked her button and held it between his lips, humming on it. Within minutes, Lydia was gripping his shoulders for support while her legs shook and tried to fold. Her labyrinth exploded with pleasure, and he licked and sucked every drop flowing from her opening.

They stepped out of the shower and briefly toweled dry before he led her to his bedroom. The mattress set on the floor looked sad and lonely, but Lydia didn't say a word about it. "God, you're gorgeous," he said, helping her down to it.

Chad laid her on her back, taking her towel and throwing it on the floor. He let his towel drop, revealing his rock hard shaft. He knelt on the mattress below her, spreading her legs wide, and trailing his hands up her legs to her inner thighs. "Damn," he whispered. "You taste delicious."

He brought his mouth back to her clit, spreading her again with his finger, sticking three digits inside this time. He fucked her with his mouth and hand until her pussy quivered again. His tongue darted into her tunnel, chasing her wetness, exploring every morsel of her while it shuddered and shook around him.

After her orgasm subsided, he ran one finger inside, lubricating it with her natural juices. He spread her open wider for a better view. Then hesitantly, he stuck his finger into her ass, as far as it would go while teasing her clit with his tongue.

She hadn't objected, and his cock jumped in excitement. There had only been one woman who had ever agreed to let him in her backdoor, but he had to stop before his full shaft was buried in her ass because she changed her mind. It was too painful. His cock had just enough of a taste of the forbidden fruit to make him crave it more. He was hoping one of these older women might be into it, and it was beginning to look like he was right.

"You like that?" he asked.

"Mmm-hmm," she moaned.

'God, this was too good to be true.'

He moved closer to her and positioned himself between her legs. He planned on fucking her hard until she came, showering his dick with enough cum to be able to ravage her ass.

"I didn't peg you as an ass play type of guy," she said.

The comment surprised him. He was young and sowing his wild oats. Of course, he wanted to fuck as much ass as he could. It seemed to be the way of horny young men. "To be honest," he said. As soon as the words came out of his mouth, he froze temporarily. *'Why are you telling her this?'* He might as well go for broke because it would be hard to come up with something on the spot when all he could think about was drilling into her. "I haven't had the chance to try it yet, but I want to."

"Really?" Her surprise was genuine. "Next time, okay? I promise."

'Next time? She already knows she wants a round two.' It made his head even bigger thinking he was some sort of sex god.

"Yes," he said, leaning into her entrance. "Next time."

They were still wet and slippery from the shower. He slid into her effortlessly. Chad raised one of her legs over his shoulder and plowed into her hard and fast. Less than a minute later, she was cumming all over his cock. The feeling was so intense. He knew it wouldn't be long until he joined her, but he hoped to bring her to climax at least once more before then.

Her orgasm gripped his cock and wouldn't let go. The throes of her pleasure could be felt over his full length as it rippled down her tunnel in waves. There was something about the way these women came. It was like a drug. It only took one time, and he was addicted.

Her next orgasm began as soon as the previous one ended, and it was too much for him. He began to buck and twitch. His rhythm slowed into slow deep strokes. His load shot into her labyrinth while it squeezed him, milking out every last drop.

After they collapsed in the afterglow and caught their breath, he asked. "So... next time?"

Chapter Five

Juggling Women

Lydia had just left after having to take a second shower. He would be seeing her again soon. She visited her mom regularly, but he had just never seen her.

'Never noticed her is more like it because I was strung up on young women who can't do half what these ladies can.'

As soon as she left, he checked the time. *'Fuck!'*

He was going to be late meeting Maggie if he didn't leave right now. There was no time to shower, no time to rinse off the scent of Lydia before he dashed out of his apartment. He barely could spare the time to get dressed, much less change the sheets on his makeshift bed.

Thirty minutes later, he pulled up to the restaurant right on time. Their little ruse worked well except for one time when a friend of hers had a few too many glasses of wine and decided to share an Uber. It was funny at first, pretending. He flashed glances at Maggie through the rear view mirror. They exchanged secretive smiles. Then her friend became belligerent and rude. He wondered if everyone in Maggie's life was like that. How did someone so naturally kind get swept up in a world where the people in it believed ninety-five percent of the population were no better than a third world country.

Maggie waved to her friends and climbed into the back seat.

"Where to, ma'am?" Chad asked as he pulled away for the

benefit of any of the women listening outside. He enjoyed Maggie's company, but he didn't like sneaking around. His days with her were numbered. It wouldn't be long before it took too much of a toll on him, but he was going to enjoy every inch of her while it lasted.

They went back to his apartment, and he couldn't help looking around nervously for Lydia. Thankfully, her mom's apartment was on the other side of the building, so there were no windows facing where he could be seen bringing another woman home. They could still run into her, or her mom. It would be quite the embarrassing scene and would probably cost him both women.

Chad was happy to skip dinner with her tonight. It was great when she cooked, but all he could think about the entire time was dessert. Getting through the meal was bad enough, but he had to wait while she cooked it too. Being grateful for the home meal never crossed his mind.

"Come over here. I'd like to show you something," he said, standing up and leading her away from the kitchen. The food was still on the table, and their dishes hadn't been cleared. It was enough to drive Maggie mad, but he couldn't wait any longer.

Maggie followed him down the hall to his room, and he stood there proudly waiting for her to notice. "What?" she asked confused.

"Your candles," he smiled. He had taken them and lined his dresser and night stand with them, lighting them when dinner was almost ready to be served.

"Oh," she said. She was severely unimpressed, but didn't let on.

Chad put one arm around her waist and brought his free

hand to one of her breasts. He massaged it and kissed Maggie passionately.

Maggie pulled back from the kiss and walked backward toward the mattresses. It was her turn to lead him. "I love how gentle you are with me when you touch me," she said. "It's sweet, but I hope you know you don't have to be. I'm not so old I can't handle rough." She laughed and lowered herself to his makeshift bed.

He wasn't sure how to take it. His intention hadn't been to be gentle. While he wasn't trying to maul her, he thought he was being at least somewhat forceful with her. *'Is this what all of my lovers have thought?'* It was the little revelations like this which infected his mind and kept him awake at night rethinking every move he had ever played.

Maggie had a flirtatious smile. One glance from her was enough to make the bulge in his pants grow. He wanted to grab her and kiss her from head to toe. *'No foreplay,'* he reminded himself.

Chad quickly unfastened his pants and stripped from the waist down. Maggie lay propped up on her elbows watching him and licking her lips. His inexperience had always told him it was a sign a woman wanted his cock in their mouth, and if she was anyone else, that's exactly what he would have done: choked her with his shaft.

She wasn't a fan of oral either. She called it an appetizer course when all she really wanted was the main dish. This would keep him awake for hours too, wondering what all this signals really meant and which he'd been interpreting wrong all these years.

"Are you going to help me out of this?" Maggie asked,

playfully tugging on her dress.

He wanted to say no. He wanted to watch her strip, but he wondered if her age and the height of his mattresses would hinder her. Instead, he leaned over her and extended his hands to pull her up. Then he lifted her dress over her head to reveal she wasn't wearing panties again. His cock jumped with excitement.

"Damn, Maggie," he moaned. He was ready. Had been ready since he picked her up. The earlier episode with Lydia had been pushed far from his thoughts, and he felt a need so intense like it hadn't been satisfied in years.

Chad kissed her again, harder this time and lowered her to the mattress with his body following hers closely. With one hand wrapped around her waist, he lifted and moved her up until they were fairly centered. There was plenty enough room for what he needed to do.

He licked and teased her nipples with his teeth quickly, finishing before she could remind him it wasn't necessary. They were so luscious and full it was hard to resist them. He positioned himself between her legs, surprised she was letting him take control this time, then pushed forward to enter her.

Chad thrust into her, feeling his cock slide in effortlessly, making her moan immediately. Before long, he was bucking into her hard, watching her juicy breasts bounce wildly as he pummeled her labyrinth in animalistic fashion.

"Oh, yes!" Maggie moaned repeatedly while he pounded her as hard as he could.

An orgasm overtook her, and her cries became louder, shriller. Her tunnel contracted around his cock, transferring her shockwaves throughout his member. When it subsided, she was breathless.

Seeing her exhausted like this from the work he had done, he felt the urge to pull his cock from inside her and slap it on her tits, rubbing the head around her stiff nipples. *'She wouldn't like it,'* he thought. *'Or would she?'* There was no time to find out now.

He pulled out and grabbed her hips, gripping them tightly. He quickly rolled her over and lifted her ass into the air. Maggie moaned, but didn't utter a single discernable objection.

Chad spread her legs open with his knee and entered her from behind. Once his shaft was buried, he smacked her ass.

"Yes!" Maggie cried.

He fucked her faster and harder, reaching under her occasionally with one hand to squeeze her breasts and pinch her nipples between his fingers. He'd take a break from her breasts and smack her ass a few more times then repeat. Soon the sound of him hitting her hard with every thrust played out a soundtrack, and he wanted to turn it up, louder with more gusto.

Chad placed his hands on her hips, pulling her to him in perfect rhythm to his own strokes.

Smack! His hand left a red welt on one ass cheek.

He brought a hand around and found her clit, rubbing it with his thumb. Maggie's moans turned into one long cry which grew louder the longer he played with her clit.

Then he pulled back and used that hand to smack the other side of her ass.

"Oh, fuck!" Maggie practically screamed. Her body tensed and began to shake. Her juices flowed out of her, drenching his shaft. Every muscle in her tunnel constricted, gripping his cock, not wanting to release it.

He wondered if he had ever heard her cuss before. Perhaps he had. Perhaps in one of their other hookups she had let something slip in the heat of passion. It was unusual for her though, and it made him feel like a king to bring her to it while he was the one running the show.

Chad continued to fuck her faster and faster. He groaned as her slippery, wet pussy clenched onto him and massaged his shaft. Then he felt the tingling begin above the base of his shaft. He was close. He gave her ass one last, good, hard smack then grasped her hips with a fierce hold and plowed her tunnel, giving her everything he had.

His bedroom was filled with the aggressive sounds of their sex. The slapping of their bodies carried the beats. Her moans provided the melody, and his grunts were becoming the lead.

It wasn't going to last much longer. He was about to cum, but he wanted to bring her to one last orgasm first. He could only hope he lasted long enough.

Maggie screamed out another climax. She shook violently while her pussy creamed all over him.

That was all he could take. He began to buck and twitch wildly. His cock jerked inside her passage as he shot his load. Their juices mixed together as they reached their peaks together.

When their song was finished, they collapsed side by side. Both of them were out of breath and covered in sweat. They lay still on their backs, occasionally glancing at the other one and smiling. It took several minutes before either of them could force out a couple words, much less move.

"Oh, I should probably get going," Maggie said when she found the ability to speak.

It wasn't what Chad was expecting. He thought he would be showered with accolades for his sexual prowess and was a little hurt when there were none.

"So soon?" he asked. "You sure you don't want to stay for seconds?" He took her hand and gently moved it toward his cock.

Maggie pulled her hand back. "No, I can't. He's been getting home early from poker nights lately," she said. He being her husband. "I haven't always beat him home. It's getting harder to come up with excuses. If he ever calls one of the girls, I'm in deep trouble."

"They won't cover for you?" That was insane. His friends would say anything to help him out if one of his girlfriend's ever called them.

She was standing now, pulling her dress on over her head. "It's not that they wouldn't," she said. "It's that they don't know they might have to. So if he were to call, they'd worry too."

"They don't... know about me... about us..." The realization hit him slowly.

"Oh dear," she said, seeing the look on his face in the candlelight.

"You're ashamed."

"I'm not ashamed of you. It's just that a woman like me doesn't do things like this. With anyone," she added. "My friends wouldn't understand."

Chad nodded, but hadn't felt so awful since a friend of his got blamed for something he'd done in boarding school. No one knew it was really him, so he let his friend take the full punishment which got him kicked out of the school. It was one of the most prestigious places to go if you wanted to be guaranteed your choice of colleges. He did feel bad for what happened, but he was thankful it wasn't him.

"Am I going to see you again?" he asked.

Maggie sighed and shook her head. "Yes," she said. "But I think we'll have to quit the poker night get togethers. We'll still have the days when he travels."

He thought about it well into the night after she left. He was being used. As much as he knew he was using her, it didn't sit right to know she was doing the same thing to him.

Chapter Six

Ass Play

It's not prostitution. Even though it can be considered a form of sexual exchange. It's not payment for services rendered. It's a trade of goods. However, his last romp with Lydia would leave him questioning that.

There were two surprises the next time she came over to shower. The water heater in the building had been fixed days before, but it was still the excuse she playfully used.

The first surprise was the bed which had been delivered that afternoon. Chad was only home for it because Lydia had asked to use his shower at one. She conveniently didn't show up until after the deliverers had assembled his new bed and hauled off the trash, including his old mattresses. When he answered the door, she was carrying new bedding.

"Don't worry. It's not used," she assured him. "I washed it for you already."

They barely took the time to put the fitted sheet on the top mattress and threw the new naked pillows on the floor since neither of them would be sleeping. "It's only right I get to be the one to break it in with you," she beamed.

It made Chad wonder if she knew he was seeing others, or if it was a guess. *'Maybe she's trying to feel me out for info,'* he thought. He wasn't going to slip and say anything he shouldn't.

He pushed Lydia onto the bed gently and grabbed her pants,

yanking them off her body. As he was about to climb over her on the bed, she sat up and placed her hand on his chest. "Wait," she said, reaching for his zipper. "I want to suck you first."

Chad didn't like to compare women. He never had, not even when he was younger and first getting his dick wet. However, this was the one thing missing with Maggie. Her lack of enthusiasm for foreplay meant oral was out. Both ways.

She undid his pants, lowering them and running her hand over his hard cock straining for release against his boxer briefs. She gripped the edge of the elastic band and lowered them down over his member. His shaft bobbed eagerly directly in front of her when she was done.

Lydia grabbed his cock with one hand and slowly stroked it. He could only stand there and watch as she played with him, rubbing her fingers over the head, exploring it as if reacquainting herself with an old friend. She leaned forward and teased the tip with her tongue while gripping the shaft. When she looked up at him, their eyes locked for a moment before she gave him a quick wink then engulfed his cock with her warm mouth.

She definitely knew what she was doing when it came to blowjobs and took her time pleasuring him. She coated his cock with her salvia, slowly taking more and more of him into her mouth. As she got used to his size, she slid down quickly, sucking hard as she slowly withdrew. It drove him crazy.

From his position above her, the view was incredible and only added to the already immensely pleasing sensation of her mouth. At this rate, he wasn't sure how much more he could handle before blowing his load. After a couple of minutes of Lydia sucking him, he was fast approaching release. He had to try to pry her off him to prevent himself from shooting down her throat. He wanted to feel her pussy around his cock before he came.

She held her ground, nudging at his hands to leave her be. She wanted to finish it, to finish him. Who was he to argue?

After he was done, they stripped their remaining clothes and laid on the bed. Chad was prepared to return the favor while he recovered until he was hard again, but she stopped him. Older women were all about calling the shots.

"I have another surprise for you," she giggled.

Chad lay on his back and waited while she dug into the bag she had dropped on the floor by the bed. When she rolled back to him, he saw a shiny toy with two wings, for lack of a better description, at the base. "A butt plug?" he asked. He was hopeful. God, was he dying to be right, but he tried to play it off cool.

"A vibrating butt plug," she said. "I remember you said you wanted to try out ass play, so I thought this was a great way to start."

"Yeah," he said, taking it from her. He turned the dial at the bottom. There were different settings. Some stronger than others. Some pulsated in patterns. He wondered which she preferred.

"This one is small enough I don't think lube is necessary," she said. She reached over and pulled the bag onto the bed. "But I brought some anyway. I've got two more in here," she pulled them out. "Each bigger than the other if we decide to go for more."

This was amazing. Chad couldn't believe how incredibly lucky he was. He wasn't getting his hopes up that Lydia would be ready for his cock by the end of the night, but if this went well, maybe she would be on their next hook up. He was finally going to have his first anal experience.

"So..." Lydia let the word linger. "Are you ready to lose your anal cherry?"

"It's like you read my mind," he grinned. He planted a kiss on her lips. He was so turned on by the prospect he could already feel his cock coming back to life.

Lydia pulled away from him and climbed to her knees. "Great! So how do you want to do this? On your back or stomach? Do you want lube? It's okay if you do. I won't judge for not wanting to take this dry even if it is small."

'Holy shit!' The blood drained completely out of Chad's face, and he felt dizzy even though he was laying down. She was planning on sticking it in *his* ass.

Chad didn't move a muscle. He was frozen in place from shock, not sure what to do. The butt plug looked small and harmless enough, but this wasn't the anal experience he was expecting. Part of him was afraid to voice an objection because he didn't want to seem naïve and inexperienced even though he knew he was both compared to the women he'd been fucking recently.

Taking his silence for consent, Lydia gently pushed on his shoulders, laying him on his back on the bed. *'Fuck it,'* he thought. *'A million gay men can't be wrong. This can't hurt that bad.'*

She stroked his massive pre-cum leaking hard-on with one hand and toyed the tight entrance of his ass with her other. The feeling was off-putting. It was all psychological. It was the knowing what was happening, what was going to happen specifically which bothered him. The sensation from her touch was actually enjoyable.

"So?" Lydia asked.

Chad hadn't heard what she said to know what to say. His eyes darted around the room nervously as if the question was written on one of the walls.

"Lube or no lube?"

"Oh," he sighed. He hadn't given it any thought. He was still trying to prepare himself for his own anal assault. "Lube I suppose."

Lydia nodded. "I get it. You don't know what to expect."

She fished the bottle of lube from her bag and poured some into one cupped hand. She smeared it all over, and he watched her skin turn shiny and slick from it. It dripped everywhere. It got on his bed, his leg, and it felt cold.

Once her hand was covered, she leaned over him again and smiled. "I'm so happy to be your first," she cooed.

He hadn't even noticed one of her hands dropped between his legs until he felt her finger touch the puckered rosebud of his ass. She wasted no time in pressing against it until it gave way to her digit, and she entered him.

"Oh shit," he moaned out. It wasn't painful. It was odd. In fact, it didn't really feel like anything if he was being honest.

"Oh, fuck!" Chad cried out. His cock jumped, and he would swear it was harder than it'd ever been. Suddenly, the sensations rocking through him were unlike anything he'd ever experienced. It was the best sexual feeling he'd ever had, but he'd never admit that to anyone.

"That's the spot," Lydia sang out. With her free hand, she began stroking him while finger fucking his asshole. It didn't take long, less than a minute maybe, until a fountain of cum sprayed out from his cock spattering onto both of them and the bed.

Chad closed his eyes tightly as if not being able to see her meant she couldn't see the red flush in his cheeks from embarrassment. He hadn't cum that quickly since his first time.

"I expected that too," she said, moving away from him.

She left the room and came back a minute later, drying her hands on one of his bathroom towels. "You haven't felt the wonders of having your prostate played with before. That's why I waited to use the toys."

It barely made him feel better. In some ways, it was worse having her vocalize his sexual immaturity.

He didn't need long before he was ready for round two. Lydia stroked him until he was hard again before readying his ass. She picked up the smallest of the butt plugs she had brought and prepared it for his ass.

Once it was snug inside of him with the base resting against his skin, she climbed over him and slowly inserted his shaft into her wet and welcoming pussy. She slid down his cock, moaning gently until his full length was buried in her.

One of Chad's legs was twitching on its own, and he worried he wouldn't amount to much this time either.

"Ready?" she asked.

He nodded.

Lydia reached behind her and pressed the button on the base of the butt plug. It began vibrating inside him immediately.

"Uhhh... Mmmhm... Ahhhrrrrrr." All he could do was elicit incoherent noises from his mouth. His mind was blank. That wasn't entirely true. It was focused on the amazing feeling in his tight ass. He didn't know what speed she had it on, but it felt incredible. He bent his knees and pulled his heels up a little, noticing it heightened the sensations.

Lydia rode him hard. He could feel the vibrations from the butt plug on his cock. That feeling was softer, but it was there. He wondered if she could experience it too inside her, if it was making fucking him that much more elevated.

Up and down, she rode him, gyrating in small circles on the base of his cock. All Chad felt was the wondrous sensations in his ass. Lydia's tight chute was an afterthought. He could feel her fucking him, but it wasn't what held his attention.

Her moans grew louder, and he could tell she was getting close. His head spun. It was too much for him to handle. Pleasure was attacking him from everywhere. He bucked into her from beneath and felt the butt plug slide around, fucking his ass as he did.

"Damn," he moaned out loudly.

Lydia gripped his shoulders with both hands, digging in her nails, and cutting his flesh.

"Fuck!" His moan was loud and shrill. His entire body tensed as he pumped an enormous load of cum into Lydia's labyrinth. Through everything else, he became aware of her tunnel constricting and tightening around his cock as she climaxed. He was thankful for that as he couldn't hold off his own release any longer to make sure she got hers.

Lydia collapsed on the bed next to him. Her breaths came in short gasps. When she was finally able to speak more than a couple of words at a time before being winded, she reached around on the bed until her fingers felt another toy. She lifted it up, showing it to Chad.

"What do you say? Want to try on a larger size to see how it fits?"

Chapter Seven

The Woman to End It All

When one door closes, another opens. So they say. Chad had never been sure exactly who said it, but the quote applied to him the day he lost Maggie. They ran into her husband on the pier, and Chad watched as the woman her husband had been having an affair with dipped into a nearby chocolate store.

He knew it was the last time he'd see her when he walked away from Maggie, and he had been right. Both of them mutually let things drop. He didn't contact her knowing she'd had a huge scare by being almost caught. If she had seen the other woman slip away, she didn't let on. He never heard from her again, but he had built up enough of a harem that he barely noticed.

Judy was taken aback when he approached her that afternoon, but only for the briefest of moments. He watched her thoughts through the changes in her facial expressions.

They seemed to say, *'Who the hell do you think you are?'*

'You're young enough to be my kid.'

'You are cute though.'

'Fuck it. I've got nothing else planned.'

'Let's see how well you survive all of this I'm bringing to the table.'

With a wicked grin, she introduced herself, and she went

back to his place that night. Her house was out of the question. Her daughter still lived at home, and there was no way she was bringing some meaningless fling by to make her daughter blush.

He'd grown so confident with the other women he'd been bringing home he didn't pause and hold his breath over what Judy might say. His apartment was coming along. The bedroom was furnished anyway. It made him relax about his bare bachelor pad.

They walked through the door, and Judy's eyes widened. "Oh my God. You have a folding chair in your living room!"

He felt his cheeks growing hot. "Uh, yeah, um," he stammered. "The bedroom was my first priority."

Judy raised one eyebrow while staring at the virtually bare room without blinking. He guessed she was regretting her decision to come by. Not only that, he was certain if all he had was the mattress on the floor still, it would've been a deal breaker.

He led her back to his room, and he could hear her sigh in relief.

"Thank God." She muttered under her breath, but not so quietly he didn't hear it.

"Priorities," he laughed. "I'll get to the rest of the place eventually."

"How long have you lived here?" she asked.

"A little over a year."

Judy's lips pursed together, and he knew she was thinking about how long it would take for him to furnish the rest of the place. The bedroom wasn't enough for her. She couldn't stand the rest of the apartment being so empty. Deliveries began the next week.

His living room was decked out first. Then she bought him

a table and chairs for the dining area. As time went on, there were smaller kitchen appliances, décor, and other odds and ends including gaming consoles for him. It was hard to be sure exactly which woman paid for what, but he skated around those awkward moments with increasing ease.

That night however, it was just him and the newest woman to add to his call list. He walked halfway across his bedroom, feeling proud of the way Lydia decorated it. When he turned back, he nearly fell over. Judy was directly behind him and already had her top off, displaying the sexiest lacy bra he'd seen on any woman over fifty.

'She was on a date with her lover,' Chad reminded himself. *'She had been prepared for sex.'*

Judy pulled him close and planted her lips on his. He pushed him onto the bed and ordered, "Watch this."

She sat down a couple inches from him and ran her hand up under her skirt. He could smell her before he realized what she was doing. It was the sweet musky smell of a woman's wetness. "Get a better view," Judy said.

Her words sounded more like a command. Chad gulped hard then moved the fabric of her skirt out of the way. Judy's hand was buried between her legs.

"Go ahead," she said. "Join me."

Chad was mortified. There was something about Judy's take charge stance which turned him on, but also provided a bit of stage fright. He was more fearful of not doing as she demanded. His cock was pressed tightly against his jeans, begging to be set free. He popped the button then slowly, and quietly as if he believed too much noise would upset her, he unzipped them. He suddenly felt very shy about the situation which was unusual for him.

He slipped his hand into his shorts. It was a tight space, but he managed. He moved his hand slowly, jacking himself next to her. The restriction of his shorts was frustrating him. He slid his other hand inside to hold the material out and away to give himself more space. It was still awkward, and he was growing impatient. He wanted to bury his cock balls deep into the pussy she was making wet with her fingers.

"Don't be bashful," Judy said, pulling on his jeans.

Somehow he managed to get his jeans completely down to his ankles without releasing his cock. He felt like it was a test of skill he had to pass if he wanted to fuck her. Everything about Judy, her presence, the way she spoke, made him feel like he was in trouble and all his actions were being judged. He continued to stroke himself inside his shorts as though modesty had instantly become important.

Judy laughed. It didn't make him feel less than he already did. She wasn't making fun, and somehow he knew that. "Allow me," she smiled.

She stood from the bed and removed his shoes, then pulled his jeans over his feet. Giving the bottom of his shorts a tug, she encouraged him to slide them off which he did quickly.

Once his lower half was nude, she unzipped her skirt and let it fall to the floor. All she had on was her bra and heels. She bent over him and ran her tongue down his cock. Up and down with her tongue a few times, then she wrapped her lips around the shaft and sunk her mouth over his member. She repeated her work until he was thoroughly saturated and wet.

Then she mounted him on the edge of the bed. Chad gripped her ass to help hold her in place. Her knees were on either side of him, and her opening caught the tip of his cock expertly without the need of any guidance. She raised and lowered herself on him with growing enthusiasm.

Her tunnel squeezed and massaged his length until she reached her first climax. She dove back into fucking him as soon as she peaked until she reached another then another.

When she rolled herself to the side and let his cock slip from her tunnel, he worried she was finished. It wouldn't be the first time he had to take matters into his own hands because he wore a woman out, but not since college. Even that was early days. If that's what this was coming to, he'd finish in the bathroom before driving her home if necessary. He learned the hard way not to wait.

Instead Judy moved further toward the middle of the bed. She stuck her ass in the air and leaned down on both her arms with her feet spread wide.

Chad scrambled up behind her and spread her ass cheeks wide. The taunt and pink button of her ass beckoned him, but he didn't feel it wise to try that on their first night together. He moved into position and pointed his tip at her opening then pushed forward. As he did, she moved her ass back into him.

He started out moving in a slow and sweet rhythm. Sliding out to the tip and entering almost his entire length with every stroke. It wasn't long until her ass started bucking into him faster and harder, telling him without words what she wanted.

He picked up speed dand plowed into her as hard as he could. Her moans told him it was appreciated. He grabbed her by both hips to steady his movements and fucked her as fast as he could. Every handful of strokes or so, he'd bury his cock inside her and stay there, grinding tight against her. Then he'd begin his rapid fire succession again.

Minutes later, he'd reached his limit. His balls tightened against him, and his cock began twitching inside her. He grunted into her one last time and released his load. There was a moan of disappointment from Judy, but he couldn't hear it over his own moans of pleasure.

When he collapsed next to her, she asked, "How's your diet?"

The question through him off guard. It was the weirdest thing anyone had ever asked him post orgasm. "What?"

"Do you eat healthy?" she asked.

He shook his head no. He primarily lived off canned goods and fast food.

"Well, I'll help you straighten that out," she said. "I know of some great meals to help with stamina."

'Ouch,' he thought. No one had ever complained about how long he lasted before now.

Judy continued to lay next to him while he relaxed and returned to normal. She didn't say anything else, but he sensed she was in a hurry to go. It was late, and he hoped that was the reason she was eager to leave. "If you'd rather, you can stay if you'd like. Beats driving this late."

"I'll get an Uber," she said, sitting up.

It made Chad feel bad. He didn't mind driving her. It was just an offer. "It's fine. I can still drive you."

She scooted off the edge of the bed. "I was planning on getting one anyway. I don't like to bring dates home. And as much as I would love to eat cum for breakfast, I have an early morning appointment."

Chad chuckled nervously. He couldn't be sure if she was

joking or being a smart ass. He was becoming convinced she had been a drill sergeant before retiring.

"You can be my new Wednesday night," she said, gathering her clothes to get dressed.

"You're what?"

"My Wednesday night. I need time away from my daughter. I love her, but it's time she settled down and moved out. It's how I keep sane," she explained.

"So you have an affair to get time out of the house?"

Judy laughed. Then she looked at Chad and tilted her head back in a full on cackle. "No. It began with a church group for the ladies. I went regularly since she was little."

She paused to slip on her heels then chewed her cheek before continuing. "That stopped after my affair with the Reverend."

Chad's mouth dropped open.

"Oh, stop," Judy said. "He was divorced, and it's not like he's a priest with the celibacy and all that."

She pulled on her shirt and smoothed her outfit out with her hands. "Anyway, I didn't go back to the group, or the church after he replaced me. I still needed some space, so I found someone to take his place."

"I see," Chad nodded. He was still reeling from her admitting an affair with a clergy man.

"So Wednesday? Work for you?"

"Yeah," Chad said. Any day would work.

"There may be a few other days when we could swing something," she said. She picked up her purse and looked around the room, making sure she wasn't forgetting anything. "Speaking of which. You free Saturday?"

Chad nodded. He felt like he was being penciled in for an oil change.

"We'll meet up. Go to the city. If you're going to be out with me, you have to dress better. I'll get you a few pieces to start a decent wardrobe."

Without another word, she left his bedroom. Chad listened to her footsteps move down the hall to the front door and waited until he heard it shut behind her. "What the hell did I just get myself into?" he asked the empty room.

Chapter Eight

Investing in the Future

"Do you know why we invited you here tonight?" His dad asked before the appetizer had been served.

"What? It's not to visit with your only child and grandchild?" he scoffed. His attitude would get him nowhere fast with either of them, but he could usually get away with a couple punches before they got too angry. Chad was growing sick of the way they constantly held their money out in front of him like a carrot, and he was the rabbit they were trying to lure into a trap.

"Fine," his granddad said, lowering his fork. "How have you been?"

"Great. No complaints," Chad said, stuffing his mouth with food. It was more to avoid having to talk more than because he was hungry. If his mouth was full, he didn't have to say anything else which would only disappoint them.

"That's it?" his dad asked. "You practically demand a social visit, but that's all you can contribute?"

Chad had leveled out in experience points on how to get under their skin quickly. At one time, he did view it as a game. If they were going to be a constant source of irritation, always putting him down, never trying to offer any support, he was going to meet them play by play. Once he mastered it, he didn't enjoy it as much.

"What do you want to know?" he asked. It really didn't need to be answered. These two were always after him about the same things. He could just never be certain which was on their mind as being the most important topics of the day. He would wait for them to ask instead of volunteering anything himself if it meant he could avoid a heated conversation about anything.

"How's the apartment coming along? Your mother tells me she visited not long ago, and there wasn't even a single chair for her to sit," his dad said.

It was hard not to show the whites of his eyes. Everything in his family had to be so overdramatic and exaggerated. "Mom hasn't visited since the week after I moved in, so no, it wasn't exactly furnished yet. There were three stools at the kitchen counter. She was able to sit just fine even if it wasn't a chair."

"And now?" his granddad joined in the conversation. "Is it furnished?"

"Well," Chad considered his answer carefully. "I suppose it could use some more... color? Maybe? The walls are certainly too bare for my liking."

"But you have furniture?"

"Yes, dad," Chad forced a smile at him. "It's fully furnished. Bedroom. The kitchen and dining room. Living room. I've even put a desk in the spare room to begin a home office."

The two men nodded satisfactory glances at each other.

'They need to visit,' Chad tried hard to stifle a laugh. *'They're probably expecting cheap quality or even used. I'd like to see their faces when they find out how nice my place really looks.'*

"How's your financial situation coming along?" his granddad asked.

'Is this a joke to them?' Chad wondered. *'They know what I*

make. Its dad's computerized signature on my paychecks. The only way for me to succeed is to ride a bicycle to work, eat nothing but cheap oriental noodles, and never used the electricity in my apartment.'

They were setting him up to fail, and Chad wasn't so ignorant he hadn't figured it out. These two men who he had looked up to when he was a child, who claimed to always have his best interest in everything they do, wanted nothing more than to break him. They wanted him to fold, to admit it was too hard, that he couldn't do anything without them holding his hand. Once he agreed to live every aspect of his life by their rules, and they grew tired of the amusement that watching him struggle used to provide, then they'd help. He'd be given everything ever promised to him. Chad refused to ever let them have the pleasure.

"Good. I mean," Chad shrugged and sipped his wine. "I suppose it could be better. But, the bills are paid, and I have food in the refrigerator. I guess it could also be worse."

"That's not exactly what your grandfather was inquiring," his dad said.

'I know.'

"What about long term financing? If something were to happen, do you have enough to cover emergencies?"

"Yes," Chad nodded. He leaned back and smiled at the waiter placing his salad course in front of him.

When he looked back at the other two men, he saw they were both staring at him, waiting for him to say more. Chad sighed in frustration. There was a price to pay for privilege. It was the lack of privacy. He couldn't do anything without either the permission of these men, or deal with the consequences of not asking first.

"I have a little over five grand in savings. Happy now?" he said, shoveling more food into his mouth. Maybe if he choked trying to avoid their interrogation, they'd feel bad for the way they treated him for once. *'Doubtful.'*

The two men eyed each other. It was a surprising amount, and both immediately wanted to ask for proof. Thinking better of it given Chad's already growing irritation, his father gave a simple nod to his grandfather in understanding. It was too high a figure based on Chad's wages and generalized expenses. Those were numbers the two men knew.

"I must say I'm impressed," his grandfather began. "That's quite an accomplishment. I wasn't expecting something so high in under a year's time."

'There's the carrot again,' Chad thought. He didn't take the bait. He didn't offer a word of explanation.

"Did you take on a second job?" his dad laughed. In their family, people with more than one income source to make ends meet were looked down upon as people who should've done more with their life at the start instead of whining about the shitty hand they were dealt. They were just too arrogant to realize that working a second job was doing something to improve their station.

"No," Chad said, shoving another forkful in his mouth. This couldn't last forever. The goal, after all, was to get the money coming to him. He had to prove himself first, like it or not, which meant this was nothing more than an exercise in self-destruction.

"I'll admit I sold a few things at first. Some clothes, games, I don't know. A few things I didn't really need any more just to have a bare minimum safety net."

Neither of them commented. They barely reacted, so Chad continued. "The rest of it came from gifts mainly."

"Gifts?" His dad sounded alarmed.

"Yes," Chad said. "Oh, and there's usually a bit of overtime every few weeks when we do month end," he added.

"What gifts?" his grandfather asked angrily.

Chad looked at him surprised. He expected them to be shocked by his savings balance. Although honestly, he thought they would be more upset he'd sold a single possession than they would be about gifts. "Birthday money mostly," he smiled at them. Each had sent him a check in a card. "Plus you know Jax just got married. I did a lot for him and his new wife leading up to the wedding. Her parents sent me a thank you in the form of several zeroes."

Their tone calmed quickly enough after that revelation. "Is it wise do you think? To leave the money in a low interest baring account instead of investing it?" His dad was always the quickest to find fault in everything he did.

"Oh, why didn't you just ask about investments if that's what you wanted to know?" Chad secretly smirked knowing this was the information they were after since they invited him to dinner. Well, maybe not investments specifically, but it was his future they wanted to control.

He wowed them with the news of his portfolio. It was by no means a staggering or even impressive figure, but considering he hadn't owned a single stock at their last check in with him about six months ago, it was certainly mind blowing. Bonds, high risk, and dividends were words he tossed around a lot while describing his assets. "Right now, my dividends aren't much," he said. "But I'm hoping to at least triple it by the end of the calendar year. This way my money can start earning me money."

Chad was pleased with himself by the end of it. Those words were the same philosophy he'd heard his dad and granddad preach about his entire life. It felt good being the one using them for a change.

"Very nice," his dad said.

It was probably the best compliment Chad had ever heard from him. He tried not to get too excited. The topic of his trusts and inheritance had to be next. It would be a gullible move to think he'd accomplished enough to receive anything now. However, he'd done far more than they expected him to do in such a short amount of time. They had to be ready to set a time frame on it, or give him a more fixed goal to achieve first like doubling, or even tripling his investments.

"There is one thing missing," his dad continued.

"That's right," his granddad nodded.

'Fuck! Now what?' Chad was tired of jumping through hoops for their entertainment.

"What's that?" he asked. His mind was scrambling to think of what he'd overlooked. The only thing not in his investment portfolio were CD's, but he had explained he had his Christmas bonus earmarked just for that purpose.

"It's about time you settled down," his granddad said.

Something about his gruff voice made his words boom and echo across the table. It wasn't real. It was Chad's fear of someday having to give up the bachelor life for good. He couldn't believe they were pinning this as a condition to receiving his money, but on the other hand, it shouldn't have shocked him if he had thought about it. Having a wife, the possibility of starting a family, a house, maybe a damn dog, these were all signs he'd be responsible with his fortunes instead of spending it on strippers in Vegas.

"That's right," his dad agreed. His dad would never say a word to cross his grandfather. Everyone knew who really wore the pants in the family. That's part of the reason why mom left. She was married to the one man who wouldn't listen to anything she had to say because he only took orders from his father. That, and the cheating didn't exactly help either.

"Jax was the last of your single friends, correct?" his dad asked.

Chad hadn't really thought about it like that, but it was true. There were a handful of others who ran in the same circles. People he'd hang out with, but also wouldn't classify as friends. "Yeah, he is," he said a bit forlorn.

His buddies had joked endlessly when Brian got hitched. He was the first of them to do so. They teased him nonstop about his exploits, or lack thereof, but the return calls and get together's dwindled after the baby came. Brian was still around. Maybe once or twice a year he got away to do something with the guys. He had always tried to convince them he didn't ever feel like he was missing out on anything. His life had changed, but for the better. He wouldn't give his family up for anything and wished he'd found his wife sooner.

Then it was Kevin's turn. Pretty soon he ditched the group to hang out with Brian more often. The scales were certainly shifted, and he was the sole one left on the single side. He wasn't going to lose any of them, but his life had grown ever quieter without him realizing it until now. If it wasn't for the women he was juggling, he'd spend most of his nights home and alone.

"You're right," Chad said suddenly. The words came as a surprise to all three of them. "It probably is about time. I just haven't met the one yet I suppose."

His dad and granddad looked at each other in utter disbelief. This wasn't the young man they expected to have dinner with this evening. This was a new and improved version of the Chad they knew.

"Well..." his dad was at a loss for words.

'That's a first.'

"Are you in the market for the future Mrs. Stockwood?" His granddad took over where his dad faltered.

"I suppose I've always been in the market," Chad thought out loud. "I mean that's what dating is, right? Searching for the one you can't stand to lose. Something like that." He cut into his steak and checked the cook on it, nodding his approval to the waiter.

The sound of his granddad's laughter hit his ears first. When he turned toward them, he saw his dad was enjoying the inside joke as well.

"What?" Chad had no idea what he said that was so funny.

"No," his dad began, pausing to compose himself. "What you've been doing is looking for the next fling. Bars, friends, hang outs, and wherever it is you meet these women of yours."

'Bridge and bingo night.' The thought came so quickly he almost choked on a bite of his prime rib.

"That's not where you meet a wife," his dad said.

"No," granddad joined in. "You meet her at the country club, or an art museum. She's someone you're set up with because her parents and yours are friends. Like follows like. If you want a beer guzzling tramp, you go to a bar. If you want a companion to support you in life, you go to where quality lives."

'Those women are boring,' Chad thought.

"I know what you're thinking," his dad said.

'Not a chance in hell.'

"Those women are boring," his dad told him.

Chad's head jerked around to look at him quickly, making his dad laugh.

"I thought so myself when I was about your age. Here's the thing." His father rested his elbows on the table and clasped his hands in front of him. "Those young ladies are just like you. They were raised a certain way and have expectations put upon them by their own families. It's not what they necessarily want and not always reflective of who they're really like. You have to break down those barriers, find the real woman underneath, and see how close she is to the person you enjoy being the most."

"Exactly," his granddad interrupted. "She can be anyone she wants behind closed doors, and that's okay because she knows how to conduct herself in public."

Chapter Nine

Christmas Gifts

Meeting Libby was pure luck. His mom had set him up in the past. The women she picked were stuffy and frigid. There wasn't a sexual bone in their bodies. Affairs were easy enough, but he'd still be expected to fuck his wife.

One of the women in his mom's building had just remarried. Her new husband still had a daughter at home, and he desperately wanted her out of the nest. It was high time she settled down and began a family. In other words, good old dad wanted some peace.

Chad only went on the date out of a sense of obligation. It was twofold. He felt a little guilty fucking one of his mom's friends in her bed, but he'd do it again. The main reason was his dad and granddad. If they heard he turned down a decent prospect for a wife without meeting her first, it would infuriate them.

They wanted him settled. A man with a wife and children to provide for was less likely to do something stupid. He had priorities like investing his money instead of gambling it away on a weekend trip to Vegas with his buddies. He desperately needed to convince them he was ready to receive the money he had coming to him.

He didn't expect for Libby to be near perfect. She was beautiful and smart. She worked as a nurse which would be great experience for raising children. They were always getting sick or falling down injuring themselves. He didn't have an opinion one way or the other about his future wife working. She certainly wouldn't have to once his dad and granddad quit being stingy with his money, but she could keep the job if she wanted so long as the children were taken care of first.

And, she did want children. So many of the women he dated had no desire to give up their wild and extravagant lifestyles. He didn't either, but having children didn't affect him the same as it would his wife. Sure, those women might change their mind one day, but what if that's what it took to get his money? He couldn't have some party girl stand in the way of it if she never got baby fever.

They were interested in the same private schools for their children to attend one day. They had the same tastes in music and movies which made it easier for dating. She had a grand sense of humor and laughed at all his jokes. He wasn't sure how his mom managed to pull this one out of her ass, but she had found the perfect woman for him.

They weren't exclusive at first, neither of them. He still had the older women who were spoiling him, and Libby dated other guys. The sex he had with Libby didn't come close to the heights he reached with his more mature flings, but sex was sex. Dating her kept his family off his back, and that's what he liked most about her.

After a while, she confessed her feelings for him and wanted to get serious. He promised her there was no one else he was interested in romantically. It was semantics. He wasn't after a honeymoon with his older women, only orgasms.

Chad would never say he was in love with her. She was

pretty, but no more beautiful than most of the other women who had sucked his dick. She talked too much. He tuned her out most of the time giving her the occasional head nod and throwing in a, "Really?" for good measure. She was someone he could see himself toting on his arm to the country club. She had good genes and came from a good family which was the only thing that mattered according to his granddad.

The time came when he knew he'd have to commit to Libby. There'd be other women throughout their marriage. It's how the men in his family were. He'd be fair to her and give her a chance to be all he needs at first before finding what was lacking somewhere else.

One by one, he began dumping the half a dozen or so flings he'd been wearing himself thin with staying on top of, literally. It was proving to be quite difficult because most of the time he tried to cut it off with one of them, some of them would offer a gift to entice him to stay. Only two ended it easily. He dwindled it down to only one on the side. Judy was a hard woman to walk away from. The sex was amazing, but the money she doled out on him was even better.

He only waited eight months to propose, discussing it with her father first as was expected of him. He decided to be cliché and pop the question at Christmas. It was selfish. The sooner he did it, the sooner the wedding, and the sooner he got his money. Plus her parents, while divorced, were both out of state over the holidays that year. Libby couldn't get the time off from the hospital to go with them. This would be a problem for their marriage, but they'd discuss it when the time came. They had her dad's mansion to themselves and broke in all the rooms in celebration. He had hoped being engaged would encourage her to try a few things, and he was right.

"What's this for?" she asked, holding a pair of fuzzy lined handcuffs. Her face was flushed from the wine, and she giggled as she tried to twirl them in her fingers.

"It's for you," Chad said.

He had brought an entire bag of toys to play with, and they had been having fun with them. There were a few he was saving for when the time felt right. Libby seemed just drunk enough for that time to be now. He needed her inhibitions to be relaxed while still fully in charge of her faculties. He wanted to take advantage of the moment not her.

"Come here," he said, reaching out his arms. She walked toward him slowly in the black lace teddy he had given her, and he pulled her on top of him on her father's bed.

"There's more where that came from," he whispered. His lips left a trail of kisses from her ear to her neck.

"Really?" she giggled again. "Like what?"

"I'll show you," he said.

Chad grabbed her and rolled her over bringing his body on top of hers. He kissed the outline of her cleavage exposed over the top of the bodice. Using his chin, he moved the fabric down exposing one breast, and he greedily took her nipple into his mouth sucking on it. One hand propped himself up, and his other hand explored between her legs. He smiled when he discovered she wasn't wearing panties. She moaned and squirmed underneath him while he teased her, brushing his fingers against her just enough to entice.

He leaned back and rolled her onto her stomach. He lifted the teddy up her back and caressed her ass. Leaning down, he brought his lips to one cheek and kissed it gently. He'd only been on the receiving end of ass play, and his cock throbbed in his shorts at the suggestion he might feel her ass squeeze his dick tight tonight. Libby wasn't very experienced sexually, and her ass was virgin territory. It made him hard as a rock thinking about being the first to defile it. "Do you know what I'd really like for Christmas?" he asked.

Libby lunged herself forward away from him and turned to the side. "Nooooooo," she said with wide eyes. Her tone was playful however, so he knew he could try again.

He let his shoulders drop and sighed. "I promise I won't hurt you."

She looked around like there was something in the room that might help her get away from the conversation. "It's going to hurt."

"I brought lube," he said.

Libby didn't say anything.

"Try it? If it's too painful, you know I'll stop. I wouldn't hurt you." He played with the engagement ring on her finger to remind her of how much she meant to him and how her place with him had changed.

She stayed quiet. She was thinking it over. Many times he had stuck a finger or two in her ass, and by her admission, she thought it felt good. His cock was considerably larger, and her friends had horror stories about their awful experiences taking it in the ass. It was because they were fucking douche bags who didn't give a shit about them. He wanted Libby to enjoy it because he wanted her to let him do it again. And again.

"You promise?" she asked quietly.

Chad swallowed his grin. He couldn't let her see how happy it made him to get his way. "I promise."

She nodded and rolled back to her stomach, inching closer to him until she was cuddled against his side.

He took his time, caressing her, and kissing her. Every couple of minutes, he'd focus on her ass, rubbing it, pressing a finger against her tight rosebud almost to the point of penetration then stopping, even licking it. He would've gone on like this for hours, dragging out the anticipation of it. His hands didn't leave any part of her body untouched, and she was practically begging him to violate her ass before he had his shorts off.

She was so turned on she didn't notice when he slipped the cuffs onto her wrists, wrapping the chain connecting either side around one of the posts at the head of the bed. It wasn't until she tried to move some time later she realized she was stuck.

He meant what he said. If it hurt too much, he'd stop. He wasn't that big of an asshole. But, he didn't want her fighting her way free the second his head entered her ass. There was going to be some pain. It couldn't be helped, but that didn't mean it wouldn't feel enjoyable too.

Chad stood up and went across the room to his bag of goodies and grabbed a few things. He flipped the light off before heading back to the bed. He wasn't much of a "sex with the lights off" type of guy, but there were some things he didn't want her to see.

He had a padded spreader bar he slipped between her ankles. It attached similar to the fuzzy handcuffs. It would prevent her from closing up on him and make sliding away from him harder. To his surprise, she didn't ask what it was or object.

He toyed with her ass again, occasionally slipping his hand down to her wet box, fingering her and rubbing her clit. Her juices were running down her legs, making the sheets wet.

Then he grabbed the lube and dumped a large amount in his hand. He rubbed it all over his cock and the crack of her ass. He dipped his fingers in it and jammed them into her tight hole, trying to fill it with lube.

"If it hurts," he whispered, "I can use more."

He couldn't see her nod in the dark, but she muttered something that sounded like she agreed.

He touched the tip of his shaft against her rosebud, and opened his mouth, but the moan he heard came from Libby. A shiver of excitement shook through him. It turned him on knowing she wanted his dick in her ass. He pressed forward until just the tip was buried in her. It was already becoming more difficult to go deeper. Her cries were high pitched and shrill. He could feel every muscle in her body tensing up.

"I'm getting the lube," he said, pulling out. He reapplied using twice as much as before. This time he kept the bottle open in one hand for easy access. "You need to relax."

"I can't," she said. Her voice was upset, but she wasn't crying.

He positioned himself again and held the bottle of lube just above his dick. He pushed the tip in and welcomed her shrieks of pleasure. He gave the bottle a squeeze, feeling the cool gel-like liquid drop on his shaft. He leaned into her, and her tight ass parted allowing for more of his cock to enter. He pulled back leaving only the tip inside, dripped more lube from the bottle and pushed forward again. Back. Lube. Forward. He repeated those actions quickly until he was almost fully buried in her ass.

Libby's cries were almost deafening, but she wasn't begging him to stop. She wasn't articulating anything. With his other hand, he reached around and rubbed her clit. It was enough to set her off.

"Fuck me!" she screamed as loud as she could.

Chad didn't need to be told twice. He dropped the open bottle on the bed and gripped her hips tightly. He pummeled into her ass until he was completely inside her. He quickened the tempo and fucked her hard, driving his cock deep with every stroke.

Her ass hugged him, tightened around him, and tried to prevent his member from pulling out each time. It was the tightest his cock had ever been handled, and it felt amazing. Almost too amazing.

He wasn't going to last long. He tried to slow down but couldn't. It made the urge to release grow, feeling the slow descent into the tight cavern of her ass, and the way her ass tightly gripped his cock on the way out. It was getting tighter now like the lube had worn off, and he knew Libby would be screaming out for him to stop soon. By the time he found the bottle again, it'd be over. He'd have shot his load.

Chad grabbed her tightly and fucked her with hard deep strokes. He tore up her tight ass, grinning at the thought of how it was no longer a virgin hole. With any luck, it would soon be a worn out hole if he had his way with doing this again and often. That thought pushed him over the edge, and his upper body twitched with the first shot out of his cock inside her. He bent over her ass while he finished shooting his hot sticky cum into her.

Chapter Ten

Wedding Dinner

It's not greed, it's looking out for numero uno. It's striking while the iron is hot. It's taking advantage of the situations that present themselves.

The only older woman left to dump was Judy. He only kept her around this long because her husband was going out of town for a week on a business trip soon, and she loved to show him off on the town and spend an ungodly amount of money on him when they were together. They'd have a whole week of her spoiling him too.

The timing both sucked and was perfect. Her husband returned the morning of the big meet the in laws dinner four weeks before the wedding. They hadn't been able to do it before then because everyone's schedules were so hectic.

He'd prepared Libby for his absence that week by saying it was getting crazy at work. He had a lot to do to prepare for the two weeks off for the honeymoon. As soon as he returned, he'd begin interviewing his replacement because his dad would promote him, and he didn't want to be too far behind when he trained someone to take over his current duties. The truth was he barely did shit at work, but he'd be busy with Judy. After the dinner, it was nothing but fittings, rehearsal dinners, his bachelor party, etc. They'd both be busy. Chad had a little experience with it from going through it with his buddies, and there wouldn't be time for much else.

Things were shaping up. His dad and granddad had already transferred some of his money to him. It was conditional, of course. He and Libby were house shopping. A new account was set up, and he'd have the rest of it deposited while he was on his honeymoon in Tahiti. The future looked bright and sparkled like the huge diamond in his fiancé's ring.

He and Judy had a wild last night together. She didn't know it was their last until the very end, and she'd probably be a little bit bitter. Didn't matter to him. Her opinion didn't matter anymore. What was she going to do? Take back the furniture she bought him? Let her. He and Libby would shop for something new. His wife should be the one picking out the décor of their new home since she's the one responsible for it anyway.

He begged her for head like always, knowing she'd say no. Most of these older women wouldn't suck a cock to save their life. It was their one downside. It was something they didn't do, or only did for their husbands, or only on special occasions. There was always some excuse.

Much to his surprise and delight, she said yes this time.

"Don't look so shocked," she laughed. "It *is* our anniversary."

Chad thought it over. He couldn't remember the exact date they met, but he couldn't believe it had been a year. The more he thought about it the more it seemed right.

"I said to myself, 'Judy, what's the one thing Chad doesn't already have that you could give him?' And it hit me. Head."

She pulled his pants down and gripped his cock with both hands. "You might want to brace yourself for this," she warned before swallowing his shaft whole.

It took less than sixty seconds for his cock to explode a load of jizz in her mouth. They were the most glorious sixty seconds of his life.

It was the best head he had ever received, and it made it harder for him to dump her. This was unfair to Libby. He should've ended all of his affairs a long time ago. She deserved for their relationship to start on the right foot.

"So," he said when she was done. "I have news."

Chad proceeded to tell her he had met someone and had just gotten engaged. Judy congratulated him, but wasn't exactly getting the hint he was ending it. "You and I both knew this would have to come to an end eventually," he said.

He'd never watched a woman go from fun loving and happy to evil wench capable of murder so fast. Judy chased him around her bedroom as he grabbed his pants and shoes off the floor, carrying them as he ran out of the house. She cussed him the entire way, throwing whatever she could grab at him. She wasn't angry that he'd dumped her. She was pissed he did it while the taste of his cum was still in her mouth.

Chad arrived at the dinner with his mom, her boyfriend, and Libby. She had already met his parents several times. He had met her dad briefly once in passing and talked to him when he told him of his intentions with his daughter. Her mom had always been too busy. Sometimes, they'd schedule something, drinks or a lunch, but she always canceled. She'd been very elusive thus far.

His family raised an eyebrow over it, but they weren't too concerned. Charles Stanton was old money. His son had done well in choosing a bride. Her parents felt similarly about him. He came from good stock, and that was all that mattered.

Libby's father arrived first. Mr. Stanton was a force in any room he entered. All eyes took notice of him, his demure stature and Chevron mustache. They also noticed the woman on his arm who was all of four years older than his daughter. She was friendly and bubbly. Strange. Manners, background, and a clear understanding of how to present yourself in public were of vital importance when you're young and choosing the mother of your children. Once you hit a certain age, you can tout any bimbo on your arm without caring what others think.

"Mom's running a little late," Libby told her dad.

"Good," he said, lifting the drink menu before motioning for the waiter.

It was rude of Grace to do this to her daughter. Not showing for several lunch dates to meet her future son in law was one thing, but this was the in laws dinner. This was one of the main checkpoints leading up to the wedding day. She should have enough courtesy to be on time.

Chad looked across the room and saw someone he recognized. He dropped his head, shielding himself with the menu. *'She wouldn't say anything,'* he thought. *'She might be mad at me, but she has more tact than that.'*

"Mom!" Libby squealed. She got up from the table and went halfway across the restaurant to meet her.

When Chad lifted his head, the room spun. He felt everything heave. His heart sank into his stomach, and his stomach fell out of his body. He wanted to hide, but there was nowhere to run. He couldn't think of a reason to leave on the spot, and it wouldn't make a difference if he had. He couldn't move.

Libby walked her mother and step-father back to their table, and he only half listened to the introductions. There was one part he picked up on crystal clear. "This is my mother, Judith

Williams, but family calls her by her middle name, Grace.

His father stood and held out his hand to Mr. Williams before nodding at Grace. She smiled coyly at him then turned her gaze to Chad. Her eyes spit daggers at him.

He couldn't believe the woman who had sucked his cock last night was standing before him at the in laws dinner. She glared at him, pursing her lips, and tapping her fingers on her husband's arm.

Chad was mortified. His face was burning red. Everyone was staring at him because he was the only one who hadn't greeted them. He was being rude, and he was sure to catch hell for it later.

Grace leaned over and whispered something into her ex-husband's ear. "Excuse me," she said to the table. She tugged on her husband's arm and led him away, toward the door.

In what was sure a very rare instance, Mr. Stanton looked around nervously. His eyes paused just enough to be noticeable when he looked at Chad. "I apologize," he said, standing up and pulling out his young wife's chair. "Something's come up."

Libby looked terrified. "Oh, no! What?" She blinked her eyes rapidly trying not to cry. "Did something happen? Is grandma okay?"

"Nothing like that sweetie," he said soothingly. "Enjoy your dinner. We'll talk later." He took his wife's arm and said, "I do apologize. We'll," he looked at Chad again, "have to do this another time."

They were halfway to the door when Libby stood up. "I'm sorry," she said. "If you'll excuse me."

"Of course," said Chad's dad.

He waited until she was out of ear shot before saying, "I wonder what that was all about."

Chad didn't say anything. He felt himself sinking in the chair, and he thought about sliding under the table.

"If you know, you better start talking," his dad said.

When Chad finally looked up, he saw everyone staring at him. He looked across the restaurant and watched Libby follow her dad outside. Her arms were waving around frantically, and he could hear the conversation in his head. *'No, there must be some mistake. Not Chad. He wouldn't do that.'*

They were all waiting on him, but he didn't know what to say. He didn't know how to say it. Finally, he said, "It appears I have, in fact, met her mom before."

There was a gasp, and his mom pressed her hand to her chest. "Oh, dear god, Chad. Please tell me you're not the latest boy toy in her life she's been going on to everyone about for the past year."

More by Darling Coxx

The Nanny Diaries Series

The Family Secrets Series

Supernatural Erotica Series

True Love's Kiss

Nightstalker

Love Potion Number 9

Spirit of Lust

Deadly Sins

Pride

Greed

Spring Break Affairs Series

Obeying Orders Series

About the Author

Darling Coxx is a seasoned writer who has been featured in many major publications under her given name. Taking a break from interviews and personal experience pieces, she is trying her hand at short novellas in the same genre she's been working in for most of her life.

Her adult entertainment career began while working as the manager of an adult store. It is her favorite position of any she's held, before or since. It was there where she made the contacts that allowed her to venture into the world of adult entertainment both in her own writing as well as producing a few pieces of her own.

Please feel free to reach out to her at DarlingCoxx@gmail.com. Follow her on Instagram @DarlingCoxx to stay updated on future publications.

www.ingramcontent.com/pod-product-compliance
Lightning Source LLC
Chambersburg PA
CBHW030843200726
48285CB00007B/2528